Molly Bang

TEN, NINE, EIGHT

Greenwillow Books, New York

Library of Congress Cataloging in Publication Data

Bang, Molly. Ten, nine, eight.
"Greenwillow Books."
Summary: Numbers from ten to one are
part of this lullaby which observes the room
of a little girl going to bed.
[1. Lullabies. 2. Counting.] I. Title.
II. Title: 10, 9, 8.
PZ8.3.B22Te   [E]   81-20106
ISBN 0-688-00906-9
ISBN 0-688-00907-7 (lib. bdg.)
ISBN 0-688-10480-0 (pbk.)
ISBN 0-688-15468-9 (Spanish pbk.—*Diez, Nueve, Ocho*)

Printed in Hong Kong by South China Printing Company (1988) Ltd.
www.harperchildrens.com

First Edition 25 24 23 22

10 small toes all washed and warm

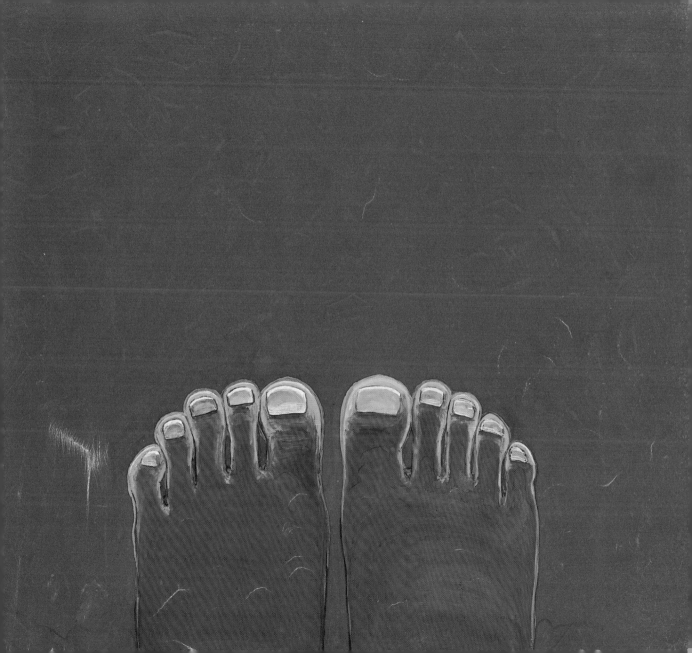

9 soft friends
in a quiet room

8 square windowpanes with falling snow

7 empty shoes in a short straight row

6 pale seashells
hanging down

5 round buttons on a yellow gown

4 sleepy eyes which open and close

3 loving kisses on cheeks and nose

2 strong arms around
a fuzzy bear's head

1 big girl all ready for bed